S0-AHE-734

I FORGOT

Story and Pictures by
SUÇIE STEVENSON

ORCHARD BOOKS New York & London

A division of Franklin Watts, Inc.

Text and illustrations copyright © 1988 by Suçie Stevenson
All rights reserved. No part of this book may be reproduced or transmitted in any form or by any means, electronic or mechanical, including photocopying, recording or by any information storage or retrieval system, without permission in writing from the Publisher.

Orchard Books, 387 Park Avenue South, New York, New York 10016
Orchard Books Great Britain, 10 Golden Square, London W1R 3AF England
Orchard Books Australia, 14 Mars Road, Lane Cove, New South Wales 2066
Orchard Books Canada, 20 Torbay Road, Markham, Ontario 23P 1G6

Orchard Books is a division of Franklin Watts, Inc.

Manufactured in the United States of America. Book design by Mina Greenstein
The text of this book is set in 16 pt. Aster. The illustrations are watercolor, reproduced in full color.   10   9   8   7   6   5   4   3   2   1

Library of Congress Cataloging-in-Publication Data
Stevenson, Suçie. I forgot: story and pictures/by Suçie Stevenson. Summary: Although Arthur the platypus has a terrible time remembering everything from his hat to the names of the oceans, he finds that there are some important things in his life which he can remember.
[1. Memory—Fiction.   2. Platypus—Fiction.]   I. Title.   PZ7.S8483Iab   1988
[E]—dc19   87-22991   CIP   AC
ISBN 0-531-05744-5.   ISBN 0-531-08344-6 (lib. bdg.)

TO PETER

Whatever he was told to remember

ZiiNG

Arthur always forgot.

"Did you wash your
face, Arthur?"

"Oops!"

Then he forgot which kind of hat.

**Off to school at last
Arthur met Nancy from next door.**

"What's with the hat, Arthur?"

Nancy was practicing the names of the oceans.

"...Arctic
...Atlantic
...Indian...
What's next, Arthur?"

"Huh?"

ARCTIC
ATLANTIC
INDIAN

"Arthur, which is the next ocean?"

"Who?"

LATER, ON THE WAY HOME . . .

"Where's your lunchbox,
Arthur?"

"Forgot it!
I'll be right back,
Elwin..."

The next day Arthur forgot . . .

...it was a school day

...his sneakers

...his sandwich for lunch

...his pencil with an eraser for arithmetic

...what time it was.

His mother and father gave him a talk...

"We're worried, Arthur."

"It just can't go on like this, dear."

So Arthur t-r-i-e-d remembering . . .

"Monday,
Tuesday,
Wednesday...
uh...
un...
Friday?"

"A, B, C, D,
E, F, G, H...
H...
K...O...
P...
WXYZ!"

"Arctic,
Atlantic,
Persifit...
Persikif...?"

He practiced and practiced.

HE TRIED REMINDERS...

...wearing a
rubber band
on his wrist...

"Ouch!"

"Maybe if I just
stretch it out
enough..."

...tying colored string to his flippers...

He tried notes.

He really tried.
But nothing worked.

Outside, Arthur stared up at the sky...